Please return/renew this item by the last date shown. Books may also be renewed by phone or internet.

🖥 www.rbwm.gov.uk/home/leisure-and-culture/libraries

☎ 01628 796969 (library hours)

☎ 0303 123 0035 (24 hours)

www.rbwm.gov.uk

Royal Borough of Windsor & Maidenhead

I CALL THE PUFFINS!

Written by
Cath Howe

Illustrated by **Ella Okstad**

WELBECK
FLAME

To Huw - C.H.

First published in 2023 by Welbeck Flame
An imprint of Welbeck Children's Limited,
Part of the Welbeck Publishing Group
Offices in: London – 20 Mortimer Street, London W1T 3JW &
Sydney – 205 Commonwealth Street, Surry Hills 2010
www.welbeckpublishing.com

Design and layout © Welbeck Children's Limited
Text copyright © Cath Howe, 2023
Illustrations © Ella Okstad, 2023

Cath Howe and Ella Okstad have asserted their moral right to be
identified as the Author and Illustrator of this Work in accordance
with the Copyright Designs and Patents Act 1988.

A CIP catalogue record for this book is available from the British Library.

ISBN 978 1 80130 036 0

Printed and bound by CPI Group (UK)

10 9 8 7 6 5 4 3 2 1

I promise to be unflappable,
To bravely cross the sea and sky,
To rescue eggs and also birds,
It may not work, but I'll always try.

LEAVING HOME

One early morning, inside her warm burrow, Muffin the puffin stretched her wings.

She opened one eye. Then she opened the other one. It must be time to wake up.

Muffin loved her burrow under the earth, full of fluff, feathers and friendly birds. It was always snug and safe.

She loved Mum and Dad's bedtime stories about a giant mystery egg that was as blue as the night sky and older than the cliffs themselves.

'All eggs must be cared for,' Mum and Dad said.

As she lay blinking in the darkness, she thought about Mum asleep by her big orange feet and Dad asleep by her head. This was home – the only world she had ever known.

Muffin's head popped out of the burrow into the breezy morning air. She hopped through a clump of pink flowers and looked down at the bright sea. Her heart hammered inside her fluffy white chest. Today was a special day. Today she would fly to the Island of Egg and start her new life in the Puffin Colony.

Mum and Dad collected fish for breakfast.

'Are you excited?' asked Dad.

'A bit.' Muffin nibbled her breakfast.

'Are you feeling nervous as well?' Mum asked.

'Yes,' she said. She couldn't eat any more. The fish kept sticking in her throat. She left some breakfast behind, and Mum gulped it down.

'Don't worry, love, put on your uniform and let's see how you look.'

Muffin stood proudly in the new uniform. The yellow backpack and the cap were amazing. The backpack felt strange, square and hard. The straps hooked over her wings. There was nothing to put inside it yet but soon it would have all sorts of useful things. The cap sat neatly on Muffin's smooth head. She tried wobbling her head to the left... then to the right.

'It's a good fit, Muffin,' Mum said.

Muffin liked the picture on the cap:

a flying puffin with the sea below.

'I just wish...' She shook her head sadly.

They all looked down at Muffin's feet.
'Stop worrying. Your feet are beautiful,'
said Mum.

But Muffin knew her feet were odd. They were orange like all puffins' feet but hers turned up at the front so it was sometimes difficult to dig with her claws. Muffin had never seen another puffin with feet like hers.

'Maybe you could hide one foot under the other,' suggested Dad.

She slid one foot on top of the other one, breathed in hard and tried to balance with her back very straight.

'That's it. Pretend you're a tree,' said Dad. 'With branches growing out of your head.'

She tried to think of branches.

'Good tree, Muffin,' said Dad.

Muffin wobbled and fell over.

'Standing with one foot on top of the other is silly,' said Mum. 'Trees have big wide roots, just like you, Muffin.'

'I was only trying to help,' Dad said pulling her under his wing. 'When I was a young puffling...'

'We don't want to hear about when you were a puffling!' Mum laughed.

Muffin pulled away from Dad's warm feather wrap.

She had another worry. What if nobody liked her?

'Remember,' said Dad, 'everyone is a bit worried on their first day, but you soon get used to it.' Dad had explained to her that, when they arrived on the island, she would have to show what she could do, 'so they can put you in the team where you fit best'.

Muffin had already decided she wanted to join the Puffin Rescue Team. Dad had told her so many times how exciting it was being a rescue puffin, learning lots of new things. You had to listen and help each other. You had to be brave. You had to be fast. What could be more fun than that? But, of course, she might not be chosen. She fluttered her wings and hopped up and down. Part of her wanted to set off for the island. But another part of her wanted to hop back down the burrow, stay at home and never come out.

Mum gathered her up in a warm feather wrap. 'Time to go,' she told her. 'And remember, whatever happens we are really proud of you.'

2

A TEST

The flight across the sea to the Island of Egg was easy. The wind was light and the sun came out.

Muffin and Dad stuck out their feet to land, right on time, at the doors of the old Shine Tower. The tower was a white building, thin and tall with a red stripe around its middle. The tower had always been here. Dad had told her about the lamp inside it that spun slowly around, shining its bright beam of light far across the sea and land.

Today, Muffin was sure she could see the shapes of birds high up inside the dome on the top. They must be keeping watch in case there was an emergency. How exciting!

An officer hopped out of the door holding a plumed pen. He wore a uniform a bit like Muffin's and his orange beak shone.

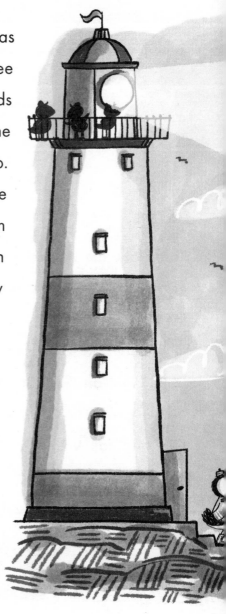

He looked her up and down and scribbled on a list.

'Name?' he asked.

Her legs trembled. 'M... m... Muffin,' she said, standing up straight and puffing out her chest.

Dad started beak-wagging. 'I haven't visited the island for years... not since I was a rescue puffin myself. It's such a special place.'

The officer nodded. 'Welcome to our ancient and beautiful island. The Shine Tower lights up day and night so we can patrol across sea and land and rescue birds in danger. Now, young Muffin, I'm going to ask you to do a few things for me. Is that all right?'

She nodded nervously. A dark cloud of doubt settled on her. What if the questions were hard or she forgot something important?

The officer puffed out his chest and pulled back his wings. 'Can you tell me what you have to do if I call "**Bird, bird, bird**"?' he asked, calling out the words in a honking cry.

'YES, WE HEARD!' Muffin called back straight away in her biggest voice. She knew this was the Puffin Emergency Call and she had been practising it with Dad.

'And what else must you do?'

'Stop everything and get ready to help,' she said.

'Excellent.' The officer scribbled something. 'Come with me.'

She followed him down a winding path to the sea.

By the water's edge, the officer pulled a white shell from his backpack. It was much bigger than most of the shells on the beach and its sides had ridges.

Muffin studied it carefully.

'Now, Muffin, I want you to dive into the water and fetch this back.' With a toss of his beak, he launched the shell into the air. It flew high and plopped into the sea, just a little way out from the beach.

Quick as a gust of wind, Muffin flew over and dived in. She felt the jolt of the cool water hitting her feathers. First through the bubbly pale blue then down into the deep darker blue, paddling with her bright orange feet, pushing hard with her wings. She passed many floating things and was nearly tangled up in long flowing weed. The current was strong and she tried hard to swim straight down. Her eyes grew used to the moving water and she kept a sharp lookout.

She thought only of that shell: white with ridges. No other shell would do.

Muffin loved to dive; her body in the water was a neat bullet shape and she could even hold her breath. The rippling blue sea was like a second home, and she knew just how to turn herself into a speedy dart, how to glide and swivel.

Past shoals of fish, slippery eels and scuttling crabs, down and down...

On the seabed, just where she had hoped, she found the white shell. It had wedged itself between some rocks. She dug it out, juggled it to fit her beak then set off back up. She burst out of the water, sped to where the officer was waiting and dropped the shell on the sand at his feet.

'Well, well, that was great diving,' said the officer. 'And no weed trailing on your wings.' Muffin's heart skipped with joy. Surely, if she kept on doing well, they would choose her for the rescue team.

'Well done, love,' said Dad.

3

FLYING

'I would now like you to collect something for me on the land,' the officer said. 'I want to test your flying speed. Please fly round the back of the Shine Tower to the exercise arena and bring back a flag that looks like this.' The officer pointed to a badge on his jacket, a flying puffin on a yellow background. 'Be as quick as you can.'

Muffin nodded. This didn't sound too hard. And he hadn't looked at her feet once. Sometimes her feet caught in the wind

and slowed her down, but she had learned
to point them as she flew.

'Your time starts... NOW!'

Muffin launched off and flapped away,
round the back of the Shine Tower, pointing

her feet, her heart hammering like crazy, saying over and over to herself, *Find the flag, find the flag.*

The flag was the same picture as the one on her cap and backpack.

The arena was a big field behind the Shine Tower. Lots of Yellow Caps were landing and taking off in little groups. Muffin knew about Yellow Caps. They were puffins who had passed all their badges. She felt so excited to see the colony and be amongst so many birds. But it was also a bit scary. Puffins wheeled all around her. She heard a cry and swerved, surprised by the flutter of someone coming in to land.

'Yellow flag...' she kept repeating, her keen eyes checking the training area. 'Don't get distracted!'

But then, she stopped mid-flap.

In the middle of the arena, sitting in a huge stone bowl, was an enormous dark blue egg.

Muffin hovered in the air. 'Never leave an egg,' Dad always said. Everyone must check an egg if they find one on its own. Here was a huge one.

Muffin was in a flutter of worry. She landed beside the giant egg and went to check. Was it warm? She laid her head against it. No, not warm, she decided. It felt cool and stone-like, just as cool as the white seashell she had collected in her beak.

But Muffin still felt concerned. Should she leave this egg on its own?

A small bird in a yellow vest popped up nearby. 'Are you doing a test? Are you looking for the flag?'

'Yes. But I saw this egg, so I landed.'

'Don't worry. This egg is our meeting

place. We call it the Midnight Egg. It's not the kind of egg that hatches.'

'Oh, thank you!'

Muffin remembered Mum and Dad's story about the huge dark blue egg that was older than the cliffs themselves, older than any bird could remember. This must be the one in their story. She hadn't realised the egg in that story really existed. She had never seen such a giant egg in her life. It was so much bigger than her. And so beautiful. For a moment, she forgot everything, lost in the beauty of this magical, gleaming, dark blue egg.

'Ahem, you'd better hurry up with the flag,' the small bird said.

Oh no! Muffin's heart sank.

'The flag's just over there. Go quickly,' said the small Yellow Cap kindly.

Muffin zoomed over to the flag wedged in the wall, plucked it out and set off back.

Dad was anxiously preening his wing when she returned and dropped the flag at the officer's feet.

The officer shook his head. 'Oh dear,' he said. He scratched something on his list.

Dad shook his head too. 'I can't understand it. My daughter is never slow.'

'I saw an egg, Dad,' Muffin said. 'A huge, dark blue egg. I flew down to check it.'

'Aha,' said the officer. 'Tell me, why did you do that?'

'Mum and Dad taught me never to leave an egg. Not for any reason. Always check.

So, when I saw the huge blue one, I thought...' Muffin felt a sob rising in her throat.

The officer waved his plumed pen. 'Listen here. You did right. You are the first new bird who has checked our beloved Midnight Egg.'

Muffin's heart rose, then fell. 'But I was too slow.'

'Yes... you were.' The officer chewed the end of his pen. 'I wonder... could you fly to that tree over there and back for me?'

Muffin took off and flew fast as a lightning bolt to the tree and back.

He nodded. 'I can't argue with that, young Muffin.' His eyes twinkled. 'How would you like to train to be a rescue puffin?'

'Really?' Muffin shook her wings with delight.

The officer drew a large tick on his list. 'Splendid,' he said. 'I think you are just right to be a rescue puffin, or, as we all call them, an Unflappable.'

Muffin couldn't believe it. It was a dream come true.

Dad's eyes filled with tears as he wing-wrapped her in a long goodbye.

Her new adventure on the island had begun.

4

THE NIGHT-TIME STORY

That afternoon Muffin joined a group of new recruits on a tour. She still felt a bit nervous. The Island of Egg smelled new and different. There were so many puffins here. How would she ever get used to all the new rules? she wondered.

The island was bigger than she had expected. It turned out to be a world of rocks, waterfalls and grass clifftops where puffins lived in ancient tunnels under the earth.

'Don't wander off. Listen and learn. No beak-wagging.'

She hopped all the way around the arena where birds took off and practised stunts and landings. 'It's so big and wide,' Muffin murmured to herself. 'And those Yellow Caps never crash into each other, even when they are wheeling in the sky.'

Next, they visited the caves under the cliffs, gathering in a huddle beside the dark entrance, gazing into the darkness and listening to the drips. The cave felt chilly. Muffin shook her wings and shuddered.

Back out on the beach, Muffin hopped to the water's edge where the sea rolled in white fluffy waves. She breathed big gulps of sea air.

Nearby on the sand were some Yellow Caps carefully untangling a net caught on jagged rocks.

'Why are they doing that?' she asked.

The officer waved a proud wing. 'They are a beachcombing patrol. Their job is to collect useful objects every day – things that have been washed in by the tide. Some are very unusual. You never know what might be useful.'

Muffin watched, fascinated, while three Yellow Caps carefully folded the net and pushed it inside a large backpack. Then they all took off into the air, carrying the load between them. Her heart filled with excitement. Imagine collecting things that might help with actual rescues.

When it was bedtime, the entrance to the burrows turned out to be full of puffins bumping and honking.

'Excuse me!'

'Coming through!'

She'd heard about the bird highways from Dad, but she hadn't realised how noisy and busy they would be. She was keen to be inside, out of the cool night air, and forgot which entrance she had been told to use, taking her chance and hopping down a tunnel.

'**Ouch!**' She bounced off the tummy of a very old puffin with a beak that looked like polished wood. He looked down at her crossly.

'Young puffins coming down must wait for puffins coming up. Or use the other tunnel. Follow the rules, otherwise we all crash into each other all day long!' the bird told her in a stern voice.

'Whoops, I'm very sorry,' Muffin said, in a fluster of feathers. 'I'm new.'

The old puffin's voice turned kinder. 'That explains it. Don't worry, we've all been new at one time or another. You'll soon get used to it.'

Muffin sighed. 'There's a lot to learn.'

The old puffin nodded. 'I understand. You are used to being in a small family. Now your family is enormous.'

A little while later, Muffin shuffled restlessly in the burrow. Why couldn't she sleep? Her mind kept drifting back to Mum and Dad and the things they always did before bedtime. She pictured her home burrow with all its familiar things. Was it only yesterday she had woken up there, ready for her first day on the island? It seemed like a thousand years ago.

Around her, she could hear other birds twitching and wriggling in the dark. Maybe some of them were thinking about their homes too.

She sat up.

A new shape appeared beside her. 'Well,' said a voice, 'I expect you're used to your mum and dad telling you a story before you go to sleep.'

It was the bird she had crashed into. Muffin realised he was right; she was missing her bedtime story. She never went to sleep without one.

'I am Kintyre,' said the bird. 'I'll tell you all a story. It will be the story of how we all came to be here. Gather round.'

All around her, out of the dark, other little puffins had started moving. They must all be wanting a bedtime story too. Muffin could feel their warm feathers and hear the rustling as everyone settled down to listen at the feet of the old bird she had met in the tunnel.

Kintyre's voice began and, just like magic, they all went still.

'Many, many years ago,' began his deep gravelly voice, 'a great storm raged right across the world. Across every sea, the wind blew so strongly that birds were blown and washed away. Huge waves smashed against the shores. Birds' cries filled the air. It was a time of terror. They were in fear for their lives.'

Muffin shivered in the dark.

'This is not a nice story,' a small voice whispered beside her.

'Don't worry, young bird. It gets better,' said Kintyre. 'A small group of puffins had set off on a journey. As the storm raged and the sea grew into huge cliffs, they were tossed on the waves. "Help us!" they cried to the empty sea.'

'Did they all die?' asked the small voice beside her.

But Kintyre sounded excited now. 'Listen

closely. A strange thing happened. As she was thrown about on the wild sea, one little puffin called, "I think I can see a bird coming.' What she had seen was no ordinary bird. This was a giant one: a bird with wings so wide they blotted out the sun, a bird with a beak bigger than the tallest cliff and wings as vast as islands.'

Around Muffin, all the listeners murmured, **'Oooh!'**

Muffin imagined that huge bird with wings stretching right across the sea.

Kintyre continued. **'Bird, bird, bird,'** cried the birds in the storm, just as the highest wave crashed over them.

And, in that moment of fear, the dark shadow fell across them, and they found themselves picked up on giant wings and carried high above the storm. It was a wonderful feeling... of floating and being gently dropped somewhere on land. The drenched, exhausted birds were all safe. In a flash, the giant bird disappeared, soaring away across the sea, leaving only the memory of its pounding wings and the bright orange flash of its beak in all their minds.

The storm gradually grew calm. The puffins fell into a deep sleep.

When morning came, these puffin travellers found themselves on this wonderful island. This island we call Egg had risen from the sea just when these puffins needed a safe place. Here was the Shine Tower with its light turning through day and night. Here were the ancient tunnels under the earth.

'This is the perfect island for us,' they all said. And so the puffins decided to stay. But more than that. 'We should do rescues just the way we were rescued ourselves,' they said to each other. 'We should care for other birds in danger just as the ancestor bird cared for us.' Kintyre's voice was warm. 'So began the story of the Unflappables. Puffin lives had been saved and we would never be the same again. We still speak and sing and remember. We still call **'Bird, bird, bird!'**, our emergency cry.'

After the story was over, all the listening puffins beside Muffin seemed to breathe out a long breath all at once.

Muffin wished she could have met

that giant bird. Imagine being one of the first puffins on the island all those years ago deciding to help birds in danger everywhere.

It was a good story. She settled down in the warm burrow. In no time at all, she was asleep.

5

TRAINING DAY

The very next day, after breakfast, Muffin waited with a crowd of other small puffins by the Midnight Egg, twitching and flapping, doing little take-offs and  landings. Today was her first training day.

An officer bird flew down and stood in front of them. She had fierce eyes. 'I am Flight Officer Faroe. Line up, all of you!' she called.

For a moment, everyone went quiet and looked at each other, heads on one side.

Muffin fought her way into the line. Someone pushed her back. A wing jabbed into her side. '**Ow!**' Everyone was shoving and jostling. Little squawks and hoots filled the air.

The officer stood straight-backed. Her chest rose. 'Too slow!' she honked. 'And too much fussing.'

She waited while they sorted themselves into a long, stumbling line. 'That's better. Let's see if you can line up next time with no noise at all.'

This officer was the kind of grown-up bird you wouldn't want to annoy. And Muffin could see she was wearing bird boots. How amazing!

'Some of you will have noticed my bird boots,' she told them. 'Only the most senior birds have boots.'

Muffin looked down at her unusual wide feet, turning up at the fronts. No hope of boots.

'You are squashing each other. Open your wings a bit. That will make a sensible space between each of you. Face me. Beaks shut, ready to begin.' The officer paced back and forth. 'Some of you have forgotten your caps.'

Muffin looked along the line. Black sleek heads, most in caps. Thank goodness she had remembered her cap this morning. She checked the cadet beside her. She stared up... and up...

'Who are you?' she whispered. This

bird was so tall that Muffin was talking to a white fluffy chest. She looked higher.

'She's quite scary, isn't she? I'm Tiny, by the way,' said a friendly head, coming down to peer at her.

'Oh... are you?' Muffin couldn't stop herself saying.

'It's funny, isn't it?' he said. 'I grew. I'm glad I remembered my cap. It's a bit small, though. It keeps falling off... whoops!'

'Maybe you could tie something round it,' Muffin suggested.

'That's a good idea. It's nice to meet you. You're the first new one I've talked to,' Tiny said.

'Me too.'

'Did you arrive yesterday?'

'Yes, did you?'

Tiny nodded.

'Now for the register,' the officer said. 'Muffin?'

'Yes, Officer Faroe,' she said.

Now the other names were called. 'Tiny... Forti... Hilly... Tenzi... Drift...'

There were too many to remember.

'And some of you need to preen your feathers and smarten up.'

Muffin shook her feathers and preened her wings the way she had been taught.

'Good. Now let's all stand still and tall. Imagine you are a cliff stretching high into the clouds. Beaks up, tails down. This Puffin Rescue Team learns to work together and help each other. We are smart and polite. Now, we're going to start by singing our Puffin Promise loud and clear for all to hear. I hope you all know your promise.'

'Everyone knows the promise,' Muffin said. Mum and Dad had been singing it to her all her life.

'I hope she doesn't make us do it on our own, though,' said Tiny nervously. 'I've been practising mine every night.'

The officer's beak pointed up and opened wide and a beautiful strong voice came out.

'I promise to be unflappable,
To bravely cross the sea and sky,
To rescue eggs and also birds,
It may not work but I'll always try!'

Muffin and Tiny joined in. The wind carried their voices far across the arena. Other puffins stopped what they were doing, and their voices joined in the song too. Muffin felt the warm power of the words.

'What do we do?'

'We rescue birds and eggs!'

'Where?'

'Everywhere!' they all called.

Muffin felt her promise deep inside her, glowing and warm. This was what she was here for. She remembered the story of the giant bird and the storm rescue.

'Now,' said Officer Faroe, 'what does "unflappable" mean? Show me flapping.'

They all flapped.

'Aaaaand stop.'

They stopped.

'When a bird is in a mess, we say they are *in a flap*, but an unflappable rescue puffin is calm and helpful. We don't get in a flap. All of you, show me some silly flapping.'

They jumped and honked and crashed into each other.

'This is fun,' Tiny said.

'Show me being calm.'

Now everyone was still and quiet.

'Flapping... calm...' They practised.

Some cadets liked the silly flapping and flapped too much every time. Muffin liked when the officer said *calm* and everyone stopped.

'You have all promised to be *unflappable*.' Officer Faroe looked at each one of them in turn. 'Hold that promise tightly in your hearts and *don't get in a flap!*'

'I do sometimes get in a flap,' Tiny whispered. 'My wings are a bit big, not like most puffins.'

'It must be useful to have big wings,' Muffin said kindly.

'Not if it's windy. I get blown into a heap.'

'Oh no, poor you.'

'It's exciting being new, isn't it? But it's a

bit strange,' Tiny said. 'I want to make my family proud of me. And pass my badges. And do the rescues.'

'Me too,' said Muffin. 'My dad was so happy when they picked me for the rescue team. He used to be a rescue puffin too.'

'Did he? So, you'll know what to do, won't you?'

Muffin nodded. 'I might know some things. My dad's still got all his badges.' She thought about Dad's badges pinned to his sash in their family burrow and she felt a pang of homesickness. 'Everything is very different here,' she said.

'I know,' Tiny said.

Flight Officer Faroe did a little growling noise and everyone was quiet again. 'Our first badge in rescue training is the

Rock Solid badge,' she said. 'We want you to get better at balancing using your wings, your feet and your beaks. These skills are very important for rescues.'

The officer led them to a big pool of water filled with tall flat things, like plates, on stalks. 'Here is our wobble board

training pool.'

The wobble boards looked like lines of flat red, yellow and blue flowers. As they got nearer, Muffin saw that the stalks were springs. 'These wobble boards can be a bit difficult until you get the hang of them. You have to take off and flap from one

plate to the next. Numbers are on the sides. Don't miss any out or you will be disqualified; you have to land on each one. And just to make it harder...' Officer Faroe flicked a switch on the ground.

'Wow!' all the cadets called, as water

jets shot up in all the gaps.

'You can use any way you like to stay on and then fly to the next plate. But if you fall off one, you have to start the course all over again. Good luck, cadets. You have an hour to practise, then I will come back and see how you are getting on.'

6
WOBBLING!

Muffin didn't think she was going to be good at the wobble boards.

'Can I be next to you, Muffin?' Tiny asked.

'Oh yes!' Muffin's heart skipped. How nice to have a partner to practise with.

They all spread out around the edge of the pool. Muffin took off and perched on a plate. She slid one foot across and tried to stand. A jet of water shot up in front of her and the plate wobbled violently. **WHOOOSH!**

She slithered off, splashing down into the water. She swam to the edge of the pool, ready to start again. All down the course she could see splashes as cadets fell off their wobble boards.

Tiny practised on the next plate along. '**Whoops!**' he shouted as he slid off and smacked down into the water too. 'This is so hard!'

They took off again. The plates were wet and slippery. Muffin moved more slowly this time and pushed her feet down hard. When the jet blasted up, she was expecting it. She dug with her claws and, as the plate shook, she flopped forwards so she was lying across it while it wobbled about. Her body slipped around and... stayed on.

Yes! Now she just had to fly to the next
one and keep going. She looked across at
all the wobbling plates stretching out as far
as the eye could see and her heart sank.
There were so many still to go.

On the next plate along, Tiny sprawled,
lost his footing and plunged down into the
water again. 'I quite like falling off!' he

called from below. 'Hey, Muffin, well done
for staying on!'

She went to answer but a jet spurted up
and she flopped off, down into the water
again. They bobbed on the water, looking
up at all the wobbling plates and birds
gripping on and tumbling off.

'It's like a battle, isn't it?' Tiny said.

At least everyone was as bad as each other.

'Again!' they both called, taking off.

After half an hour they could both flap from plate to plate and hang on even when the jets of water shot up. Muffin hadn't fallen off a plate for ages. Having curled-up fronts to her feet was useful, she realised, for when she was lying across a plate, because she could hook her feet around the edge of the plate, just for a second or two.

Tiny used his wings a lot to stay on.

'Normally, my wings are too wide and flappy but today they are just right,' he said, clinging on to a wobble board above her.

Watching Tiny holding on above her gave Muffin an idea for a game.

'Count down three... two... one, and then let go of the board,' she said. She pulled on the spring under his wobble board, bringing it towards her as far as she could.

'Three... two... one!' Tiny shouted.

She let go of the spring.

Tiny flew off the plate and sailed through the air, splash landing on the other side of the pool.

'It's a puffin whizzer!' Tiny said in delight, flying back to meet her. 'Can I whizz yours next?'

Puffin whizzing was really great.

'My head is spinning,' Tiny said as they bobbed around in the pool together afterwards.

'I quite like being thrown off now,' said Muffin.

'Me too,' said Tiny.

Muffin realised she hadn't been homesick at all since she had started playing with Tiny. She'd been having too much fun!

7

A REAL EMERGENCY

Three whistle blasts sounded from the Shine Tower and everyone looked up. All the Yellow Caps nearby stopped what they were doing.

The emergency alarm!

'Is that for us too?' Tiny asked. 'It's not a trick, is it?'

'I think we should go to the Midnight Egg,' Muffin said, shaking her feathers.

The sky filled with calls and flapping.

The Yellow Caps blew their whistles as they landed.

'**Bird, bird, bird!**' called a voice.

'Yes, we heard!' everyone called.

Muffin joined in.

What could the emergency be? she wondered. Who would be sent to help?

A thin old bird with a proud orange beak perched on the edge of the giant stone bowl. She closed her wings. A hush fell. They waited.

'I am Commander Tench.' Her voice was solemn and deep. 'I have to tell you that all training must stop. A baby bird called Minchie has disappeared in a gust of wind while practising flying. He has been gone the whole day and must be found.'

All the puffins were nodding, calling, **'Yes, we heard!'**

Commander Tench stood very still as she spoke. 'This chick is only a few weeks old.'

'Only a few weeks. The poor wee thing!' said a nearby puffin.

'Minchie was last seen with his family in Bonniewee Forest,' the commander went on. 'That is where our Yellow Cap teams will begin their search. As you know, baby birds often fly in the opposite direction when they get panicky. So, this chick could be anywhere. We need you all to get out there, join in and bring him safely home.'

Hoots of agreement sounded.

Their teacher, Flight Officer Faroe, called,
'Muffin, Tiny, your job is to look for this baby
bird here on the island. Check behind every

rock. Hunt through each clump of grass. But make sure you stay close beside the Shine Tower and don't go near the cliffs: that area would be far too dangerous.'

'We will!' they called. Then the flight officer flew away.

Muffin and Tiny watched her join the magnificent team of Yellow Caps streaming silently across the sea. Light from the

Shine Tower beamed across their backpacks every thirty seconds before the darkness came again.

'Don't they look amazing? One day, that will be us,' Muffin said.

They started hopping around the side of the tower, keeping a sharp lookout for anything unusual. It was strange being out here in the dark. Cadets were roaming the whole area. Muffin could hear their hoots and calls.

Sea mist rose as night fell. The air turned cooler. Muffin shuddered. As she searched, her head filled with thoughts of that poor lost baby, Minchie. Being lost was horrible. One day, when she was very small, Muffin had got lost herself. She remembered that lonely chill worse than winter. She had only

been a very young puffling and had come toddling out of the family burrow following the wrong parent bird and found herself outside alone. Then she'd panicked and got tangled in some long grass. She hadn't even called or tried to find her way home, just lay there with her feet in the air and her heart pattering. It was Mum who had come searching for her. She would never have found her way back herself.

Tiny gazed out to sea. 'Minchie could be anywhere. Birds get blown off course all the time. He could be right here on the island. Or he could be miles and miles away,' he said. 'It's very dark, isn't it?'

They hopped all the way around the back of the Shine Tower, checking every boulder and clump of grass. At least they were together, Muffin thought.

'Shall we sing?' Tiny asked.

'Good idea,' Muffin said. 'My mum and dad have a thing they sing to stop worrying and cheer themselves up. It goes like this:

> *Shake your feathers,*
> *it's a brand new day. That's how*
> *you blow your worries away.'*

It didn't seem right to sing loudly so they sang it softly.

'The words sound wrong,' Tiny said thoughtfully. 'It's not a brand new day, is it? It's not day at all.'

He was right.

'Oh, no, I suppose it isn't,' said Muffin.

'I know, let's change it. We can keep *shake your feathers*. That's still OK. *Shake your feathers, it's the darkest night,*' Tiny sang.

'*When you're with a friend, you'll be all right,*' Muffin said.

Her heart skipped. She had thought of the extra words so easily.

Tiny laughed. 'That's so clever. It doesn't seem so dark now we've found the right words. It seems... it seems to have brightened up a bit.'

'Yes,' Muffin's heart felt warm. 'Yes, it does.'

'*Shake your feathers, it's the darkest night. When you're with a friend, you'll be all right!*' they sang.

'That must mean we're friends now?' said Tiny.

'Yes,' said Muffin. 'Yes, it must.'

They came out on the side of the tower that looked out over the sea and felt the wind catch in their feathers.

'Whew! It's much more windy on this side,' Tiny said.

They began to search though the grass, singing as they went.

A little way below them, somewhere on the cliffside, a small sound began, carried on the wind. Muffin paused to listen.

It was coming from a little way down the steep rocky slope... A wail, wobbly and shrill... then silence.

Muffin sensed Tiny twitching. He had heard it too. 'That noise was just the wind, wasn't it?' he said.

WhoOOOSh WhoOOOSh

Sometimes the wind made odd noises.

It was blowing strongly now, whooshing around Muffin. She caught the little sound again, a high tweeting. **Tweeeet**

'There's definitely something there,' she called. 'I think we should check.'

'We can't, Muffin. It's too dark to go down there,' Tiny said. 'The flight officer said not to go on the cliffs.' Tiny's voice was full of worry. 'My wings don't like high winds. We could get blown off. Maybe we should wait for a while?'

Muffin wondered what to do. 'What if no one else comes? If it's an emergency, do you think we are allowed to go?' she asked.

The little cry sounded again, more urgent now.

She made up her mind. 'I'm going to check a bit further down the cliff.'

'Oh, Muffin, do you think that's safe?'

Muffin thought of the story of the

giant bird and his brave rescue in the storm. She thought of her promise: *It may not work but I'll always try.*

'You wait for me here, Tiny,' she said. 'I have to do this.'

ON THE CLIFF

The beam of light from the Shine Tower lit up the sky... then darkness fell again. Muffin followed the cries, perching and fluttering. The beam of light spread again. She looked over the rocky cliff edge. A gust of strong wind tugged at her. The sea roared below. **Meeep!**

'Hello!' she called.

'Meep!' went the noise.

It was a bird.

Muffin edged out onto a rock then slid down the slope, spreading her feet in front of her. Pebbles rolled away into the darkness.

'Who's there?' she called.

The beam lit a bundle of feathers on a ledge down the slope below her.

She gasped, slid faster and stopped beside the fluff ball. The baby bird at the back of the ledge was shaking and fluff was blowing in all directions. A pair of big eyes shone up at Muffin.

'Hello,' Muffin said gently. 'What are you doing here, little one?'

'We were all flying, then a big cloud came, and I got lost,' said the little bird. 'Where's Mum and Dad?'

'Are you Minchie?' she asked.

'Yes.'

Muffin called up to Tiny. 'I've found Minchie.'

'Can I help?' he called. 'Do you want me to come down?'

Muffin thought about Tiny's wings. 'It's too windy,' she called back. 'Stay there.'

Muffin liked the sea. She had never been scared of the cliffs, as some birds are. But she knew the dangers.

'Can you fly a bit?' she asked softly, moving as near the chick as she dared.

'No,' said Minchie. 'I feel all wobbly.'

'Maybe you could walk, if I walked with you?'

'I'm too tired,' said the baby in a shaky voice.

Baby birds weren't sensible. They couldn't think properly, Mum always said.

As she listened to the pounding waves down below, Muffin imagined the little puffball bouncing away down the slope into the foaming sea. She looked up into the sky for Yellow Caps returning, but the sky was empty.

Panic rose inside her. How could she get this chick all the way up to the top of the slope?

'Could you try and walk?' she asked Minchie.

Minchie reached out to her. 'My legs won't work.'

Muffin tried to grip the slippery rock with her claws and wrapped her wings around him. Then she had an idea. 'Climb on my feet,' she said. 'Come on. Climb on.'

Minchie wasn't heavy but it was hard to balance. Muffin turned to face the rocky slope. Slowly, she set off back up the cliff with her fluffy bundle, through clumps and crevices. Her foot slipped. She slid back down to a spiny bush. '**Ow!**' she called.

'**Ow!**' cheeped Minchie. 'Something spiked me.'

She gathered him to her again and they started back up the slope. 'Keep holding on!' Muffin gasped, her wings like a cloak around the chick. She held on

to a trailing root with her beak, pulled on it, shuffled upwards, found another one and pecked again.

Mum and Dad's voices echoed in her head. *You can do this!*

She had never felt so tired. The top of the cliff seemed so far away. Minchie felt heavier and heavier. And it was hard to stop him slithering off her feet. 'Don't let go. Keep holding me,' she told him. All Mum and Dad's sayings flooded her mind... *Strong heart, good place to start... A Yellow Cap never takes a nap...*

Muffin's breath came in tiny gasps. She stopped for a moment.

'Someone's singing,' said Minchie.

They listened. From the top of the cliff a voice was singing.

> *'Shake your feathers,*
> *it's the darkest night.*
> *When you're with a friend*
> *you'll be all right.'*

'That's my friend Tiny,' she said.

'Can we sing it too?' Minchie asked.

'I haven't got enough puff to sing,' Muffin panted.

But she did feel better. Somehow the sound of Tiny's singing gave her wings and feet a new power and she pushed on up the steep cliffside.

But as they got near the very top, Muffin realised there was nothing to hold on to on the slope above her. She quivered, her feet beginning to slither and slip. Oh no – she would fall back down. She might even end up dropping all the way down into the sea with her little bundle. Or hitting the rocks as she fell. How terrible! She gulped.

She felt like crying. She had run out of puff and strength and just about everything.

But then, when she looked up next,

two dark shapes stretched down almost to where she was. Hope surged inside her. She recognised them. Wings. Tiny had spread himself face down and stretched his long wings to meet her. She reached up and locked her wings into his. Slowly, she felt him begin to pull. Inch by inch, she was moving up towards the top of the slope.

'Keep going, Tiny,' she panted. 'Don't stop!'

There at last was his face and fluffy head. 'Muffin! I've got you,' called his familiar voice.

'Don't worry. I won't let go.'

Her heart soared as Tiny pulled her over the top to safety. 'This is Minchie. Say hello to my friend Tiny,' she said.

Between them they had saved the little chick. They'd done it. Everything was all right.

CELEBRATIONS

A special bed was found for Minchie in the nursery while his family was told the good news.

The next day Muffin's team did their wobble board test for the Rock Solid badge and the flight officer told the team that they had all passed. 'I notice you've all discovered puffin  whizzing. This can be very fun but also rather dangerous. Please don't pull back too hard on the springs because yesterday a puffin ended up being shot right out of the pool, knocking over an officer.'

In the afternoon, a wonderful ceremony was held. All the colony came. The day was warm and sunny. Mum and Dad were in the front row, and Dad was wearing his sash with all his badges on it.

Muffin stood beside Tiny and her chest swelled with pride as Commander Tench made a speech. 'These two young cadets show all the makings of great Yellow Caps. I present you, Muffin, and you, Tiny, with your Rock Solid badges and your Special Bravery Awards for the rescue on the cliffs.'

At the back of the crowd, Muffin could see Minchie waving with his family beside him. Muffin waved back.

All the birds stood singing their promise, their beaks pointing to the sky.

'I promise to be unflappable,
To bravely cross the sea and sky,
To rescue eggs and also birds,
It may not work, but I'll always try.'

'Remember,' the commander said, 'we are all made differently. That's what makes us special. Small and larger feet. Different kinds of wings. These two young cadets used their intelligence and worked as a team. Well done, Muffin and Tiny!'

Muffin looked down at her unusual orange feet with their turned-up fronts. She had decided she didn't want bird boots after all. She didn't want bird boots AT ALL!

When all the badges and medals had been given out, all the puffins were free to find their friends and families.

There's another surprise I never told you about,' said Dad as he and Mum came up and wing-wrapped her so

tightly, she thought they would squash her completely. 'Unflappables celebrate in the best way ever! Come and join the splash.'

And that's when the huge dish around the Midnight Egg turned out to be a giant bird bath. Water flooded in, making swirling fountains and frothing whirlpools. There were so many games you could play. The whole colony stayed up late into the evening celebrating. Muffin and her new friend Tiny leaped, dived and splashed each other in a spectacular display of joy.

'I love being an Unflappable!' Muffin called. 'It's the best job in the world!'

THE END

FACTS ABOUT PUFFINS

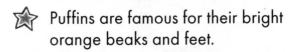 Puffins are famous for their bright orange beaks and feet.

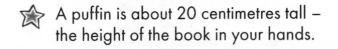 A puffin is about 20 centimetres tall – the height of the book in your hands.

They live on the coasts of North-west Europe, eastern parts of North America and the Arctic coasts such as Greenland, Iceland and Scandinavia. They spend six months at sea every year. On land they live in burrows.

 They weigh about 600 grammes – a bit less than 2 cans of fizzy drink.

Puffins have one chick called
a puffling.

 Puffins eat plankton and fish.

Puffins beaks light up in the dark.

 A place where puffins make
their home is called a colony.

For more information, please visit
The RSPB Wildlife Charity: **www.rspb.org.uk**

About the Author:

Cath Howe is an author and a London teacher. She loves helping children with creative writing in schools. She grew up in Scotland and spent many holidays in remote island places watching the seabirds and collecting things she found on the beaches. Cath is known for writing stories with a big heart. She fills her notebook with ideas everywhere she goes. Cath would love to be unflappable.
Find out more at: **www.cathhowe.com**

About The Illustrator:

Ella Okstad is an illustrator living in Norway. She loves to draw all sorts of different things such as puffins, invisible cats, humans and not so scary monsters. She has worked on lots of different children's books for both Norwegian and British publishers and is particularly well known for illustrating the Squishy McFluff series.
You can visit her on **www.okstad.com**
or Instagram **@ellaokstad**

Look out for the next adventure:

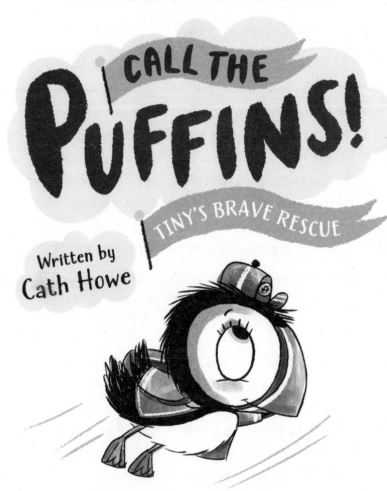

CALL THE

PUFFINS!

TINY'S BRAVE RESCUE

Written by
Cath Howe

Illustrated by Ella Okstad

Flying into the world in October 2023.